CYBER FEVER

Gillian Philip

Evans

VISIT OUR WEBSITE www.evansbooks.co.uk

First published in 2010 by Evans Brothers Limited
2A Portman Mansions
Chiltern Street
London W1U 6NR

British Library Cataloguing in Publication Data
Philip, Gillian, 1964-
    CyberFever. — (On the wire)
    1. Online chat groups—Juvenile fiction. 2. Children's stories.
    I. Title II. Series
    823.9'2-dc22

    ISBN-13: 9780237542627

Series Editor: Bryony Jones
Design: Calcium
Photography: Shutterstock

Chapter One

>LOL! That was a good one - u told him! ☺

    Mamie grinned at the direct message on her screen. Yeah, she was kind of pleased with that last posting too. A little bit snarky, a little bit funny, didn't make her look like a complete bitch but left lucas_fan nowhere to go. She'd kind of had a feeling sam12 would like it. That had been in the back of her mind when she made the remark. Not that she was trying to impress him. Just... she'd known it would appeal to him. That was all.

And she liked making sam12 LOL.

She clicked back into the main FilmFever chat room, running her gaze down the last few postings. Nope: no sign of lucas_fan. Off licking his verbal wounds, no doubt. There was a new comment from sam12, though.

>**Yeah, i'm with mamie_blues, she knows what shes talkin about. unlike some LOL!**

>**Hahaha!** added someone else. >**ur right but lucas_fans a BIG lucas fan thats the trouble right?!!?!**

About to reply on the thread, Mamie changed her mind. She opened up another direct message to sam12 and typed:

>**Thanx!** ☺

Biting her lip, she hesitated. Then she added:

>**Thanx. ur sweet!** ☺

Clicking 'send' before she could

change her mind, Mamie sat back in her chair and swung it gently left and right. Maybe that was a bit – what her nan would call 'forward'. But hey, it was no more than the truth. Sam12 *was* kind of sweet. Always backing her up, always saying she was smart, that she knew a lot.

After all, she *did* know a lot. She might not know as much as she should about the GDP of China or the origins of the First World War, but on her own subject she was so hot she was smoking. She'd rather watch movies than soap operas any day or night. She liked even the quaint old black-and-white ones that filled a Saturday afternoon or a sick day off school. More than once she'd quietly switched on the TV at one in the morning to watch the late-night horror or art-house movie they refused to show in primetime, then got yelled at for sleeping in in the morning. As for her subscription to

that DVD rental service, she must be really skewing their statistics. Their accountants probably hated her. Or so sam12 had told her last week, admiringly.

She got it from her dad. She'd been watching the late night shows since before she could remember, since he'd switch them on when it was his turn to get up and feed her. Right up till Mamie went to school, when Dad had been out of a job and it was her mum who'd gone out to work while he stayed home and looked after her, the pair of them would sit watching his DVD collection. It was what they both liked best, after all, and she'd loved curling into his lap, hiding her face in his shoulder at the scary bits (not too scary – he was careful that way) and giggling her head off with him at the funny parts. And Dad knew a lot about movies, too. He knew scandal about the stars, he knew about the studios' history, he knew how they did the special effects and he could tell you which technicians had done which ones.

That was what she'd missed most when she went to school, those afternoons cuddling up to him while they got lost in another world. Of course she'd missed it even more after he left.

Yep, she got her love of films from her dad, all right. Which was probably why her mum disapproved.

Just as she thought it, her mother's blonde head appeared round the bedroom door. 'Mamie, are you–?' She frowned. 'You're not on that laptop again?'

Just as well she had learned to click the minimise button, and fast. The screen was now filled with a tedious report on *Romeo and Juliet*. 'I'm doing my homework, OK?'

'Oh. OK, then.' Her mother smiled. 'You ready for something to eat?'

'Nearly.' Mamie glanced back at the screen, fingers itching for the touchpad. 'Just let me finish something?'

'Don't be long.'

As soon as her mother had disappeared, Mamie clicked the chat room window open once again. Just as she'd expected – no, as she'd hoped – there was another direct message from sam12. Not about films this time, though.

>**So is Mamie ur real name???**

Mamie smiled to herself. She got that question a lot, though not usually in a chat room. People usually didn't ask.

>**Yeh, i know, weird!! Some old blues singer my dad liked**

>**I like it, its nice**

She hesitated only a second. >**And ur real names Sam?**

>**Yes, not as pretty as urs, eh?!**

>**I like it too. Got to go**

>Shame ☹ hope u didn't mind me askin

>No, just got to go or i'll be in trouble! ☺

>OK, oops! Ur parents calling u?

>Just mum, T's ready. C u later tho...

Pushing back the chair from her desk, she stood up, feeling oddly nervous and excited. Sneaking off the chat room to have a secret word with each other felt a bit like flirting. Which was OK, really. There wasn't any harm in it at a distance... and anyway, she had a feeling she wouldn't mind flirting with sam12 in real life. He was only a couple of years older than her, and though she'd never seen a photo, he sort of *sounded* cute.

Not that his appearance, sound or cuteness was relevant. Since she wasn't ever going to meet him in the flesh.

Chapter Two

'Mamie, you haven't done your report on *Romeo and Juliet*?'

Oh, damn. Guilt squeezed her, more at the tone of disappointment in Mr Mulgan's voice than at her own failure. How could she have forgotten the thing? She'd actually looked at it on the screen last night and thought I'll do that in a minute when I've answered miz_biz's question about *Sleepy Hollow*... and of course it had gone right out of her head. It wasn't like she couldn't have

written a perfectly good report
either; she'd seen the Baz
Luhrman movie often enough.
　　'I'm really sorry. I'll bring
it tomorrow,' was all she
could say, lamely. Mamie
was aware of the rest of
the class watching her,
some of them
enjoying her
moment of
shame. It
was true

that she used to be Mr Mulgan's favourite, so this was kind of her comeuppance. She never used to forget homework. She knew, with a vague unease, that she'd forgotten the stupid report because she was distracted by FilmFever. Well, it had been a fascinating discussion, and she knew *loads* about Johnny Depp *and* Christopher Walken. No way could she have let them go on talking without her. It would have been a downright dereliction of duty.

Not that it was more important than homework, but...

'Well, if you make sure to bring it in tomorrow. This isn't like you, Mamie. Wait behind after class, will you? I'd like a word.'

She nodded, but she'd only half-heard him, and she found it easy to ignore the snickering of the two boys behind her. The fact was she'd remembered something sam12 had said last night, and she'd just thought of something really clever to add, something that would really make him laugh. She imagined she could actually hear him laughing, in real life, and she felt a pang of regret that she probably never would. Cute. Sam12 was sweet *and* funny.

Maybe Mr Mulgan had seen the smile flickering on her face and misinterpreted it, because he was pretty cold with her after class. Was anything bothering her? Anything she didn't understand about the work? Anything wrong at home? How was it going with her parents' divorce?

All rather personal questions, in Mamie's opinion, but she might have opened up a bit more if he'd been less frosty. The work was fine, her parents were getting on as well as might be expected, and all was well with the world.

Trouble was, she hadn't really focused on what he was saying, so desperate was she

to remember that comment for sam12, word for word. After all, she could remember what he'd said that way: exactly, word for word. And she was pretty sure his snippy comment to the flirty dodge_city had been a shot across the other boy's bows, just to warn him off Mamie. Mamie didn't care if that was chivalry or possessiveness. Either one was fine with her.

When the teacher finally dismissed her – with rather a disapproving look, she couldn't help thinking – Nicky was waiting for her in the corridor.

'So what did he say?' Nicky tucked her hair behind her ear and grinned. 'Did you get a rocket up the backside?'

'Nah.' Mamie grinned back. 'Mild ticking-off. I'll do it for tomorrow and he'll love me again.'

'Oh yeah? Like last time.' Nicky nudged her as they turned to walk towards the main glass doors, and faked a bad American drawl. 'You're walking the line, girl. Livin' on the edge.'

'Uh-huh.' So it wasn't actually the first time she'd forgotten her homework in the last couple of months. Well, she needed to relax a bit. The work had been getting really intense, what with exams being on the horizon. She couldn't go on obsessing about schoolwork; she'd burn out before the exams if she wasn't careful.

Better to obsess about sam12 anyway... a smile flickered on her face.

'Oi, is that dirty thoughts going through your head?' Nicky laughed and dragged her through the doors and out into the school grounds. 'Tell me you fancy Mr Mulgan...'

'Oi, get stuffed!' Laughing, Mamie swung her bag at her. 'Forty if he's a day. Go jump in the ditch.'

'See? Mooning over the man.' Nicky batted her lashes and clasped her hands. 'You need to forget him. Come on and we'll catch the cafe before it shuts.'

Mamie hit her hard in the ribs with a well-placed elbow. 'Shut your face. I can't go into town, I've got to go home. Blame the Montagues and the Capulets.'

'Hey, you're kidding.' Nicky had sobered very suddenly. 'You said yesterday you'd come. I need to get new jeans, remember? You were going to help me shop.'

'Yeah, well, that was before Mulgan caught me. Got to do this stupid report, haven't I?'

'That won't take all night! You told me you'd done two-thirds of it.' Nicky's face had darkened to a frown now.

'Still got to get it done, I mean–'

'You promised. You said you'd–'

'Yeah, well, I *can't*,' said Mamie stubbornly. 'If I don't hand this in in the morning he'll do his nut.'

'Whose fault is that? If you'd done the stupid thing when you were supposed to—'

'Look, I'm sorry, OK?' Mamie came to a halt. Nicky sounded genuinely upset, and she tried to sound more apologetic. 'I'll come on Saturday if you want.'

'I'm working on Saturday.'

'Monday after school, then. I *promise*.'

'Yeah, and how much is that worth? You know what?' Nicky sounded really furious now, and Mamie couldn't help thinking how much Nicky hated being let down. Phobic about it, really, because her parents were always doing it to her, too. 'I bet you spend half the evening on the web anyway. I bet you don't even start that report straight away. I bet you go online and onto one of your stupid groups. That report'll take you half an hour to finish, max. You do *not* have to go home right now.'

Mamie stiffened, stung because she was guiltily aware Nicky was right about her intentions. 'I *do* have to go.' And anyway, she managed not to add, we'd hardly have a lovely time in each other's company now, would we?

'Suit yourself.' Nicky turned on her heel and strode off. Mamie was about to yell after her to get over herself, and yeah, OK, she'd come to town after all. Because Nicky was right about the report, and it would really be stupid to rush home just to impress a boy she hadn't even met yet. She and Nicky could make it up over a caramel mocha in the cafe and then have fun shopping, and she'd still be home in plenty of time to finish the wretched *Romeo and Juliet*.

But it was all too late. Nicky was nearly 50 metres away and had fallen into step with Martine and Becca, who Mamie didn't even like that much.

'Fine,' she muttered. 'Get your jeans on Becca's advice. And see if they fit.'

So that was fine. Fine. She could go home and chat to sam12 with a clear conscience.

Chapter Three

>**Hey, dont worry about it, she'll forgive u**

>**Yeah I know.** Mamie flexed her fingers, wondering how to express her guilt about Nicky without sounding bitchy, and without letting on that it was essentially sam12 who'd caused the quarrel. Best to move on, really. >**So what u seeing tonight?**

>**Late show, sci fi double bill. U?**

>**Nothin special. Might watch Avatar DVD again.** Mamie hesitated. This was usually the kind of stuff that would start a discussion

on FilmFever, but for some reason she didn't feel like strutting her stuff in the chat room tonight. Still feeling guilty about Nicky was undoubtedly part of it. Being consoled by sam12 was definitely another part.

>**DVDs good but not the same as big screen**

>**Yeah but nearest cinema 20 miles away** ☹

>**O no! U don't get there a lot?**

>**No. DVDs mostly**

>**Shame. Where u live?**

Mamie let her fingers trail over the keyboard. It was exactly what her mother had told her not to do – well, what everyone said not to do – but this was sam12, for heaven's sake, not Charles Manson.

She played for time. >**In the sticks. U?**

>**Not quite the stix. Not huge but at least weve got a multiplex LOL! So u in the north? South?**

>Kind of both, LOL! Dads a bit further north. Cheddingham

>Ur kiddin, I'm in Edgerton

Oh, she could hardly let that go.

>Edgertons just down the rd from dad!!

>U cant be that far away from him?

>100 miles-ish

>Oh right. U don't c him much then

>1x a month which isn't bad. Hes really into movies, thats what got me started!!

>Oh OK, so he comes to pick u up?

>Nah I go down on train & he meets me

Mamie sat back and bit her lip, watching the screen for his response. The next suggestion was obvious, really. The train went right through Edgerton, after all. And would she take him up on it?

Yeah... yes, she would. Meet up for a coffee, why not? Maybe she should suggest it herself. Sam12 himself seemed to be hesitating – probably wondering if she'd take fright and think he was a crazy stalker – so she could make the suggestion herself. Nothing to stop her...

>Hey u looked at FF in the last minute! Lucas_fan's back & makin a nuisance of himself!! LOL!

Mamie blinked, so taken aback she nearly knocked over her Coke Zero. She caught it and steadied it, surprised at how disappointed she felt. Hurt, almost. When she clicked onto the chat room, sam12 was already having a go at lucas_fan, and clearly expecting her to join in. Had she misread all his signals or what?

>Is mamie_blues there?? What do u think?

She smiled at the screen. He was pulling her into the conversation, demanding her opinion. So it wasn't as if he wasn't talking to her. And to be honest, his reaction had been kind of reassuring. Of course it was stupid to start giving out personal details and getting into intimate conversations. He knew that as well as she did, and he

was the one who'd pulled back. Which was kind of nice.

>**Yes I'm here, cant believe u just said that lucas_fan! I got 3 words for u: jar jar binks!!**

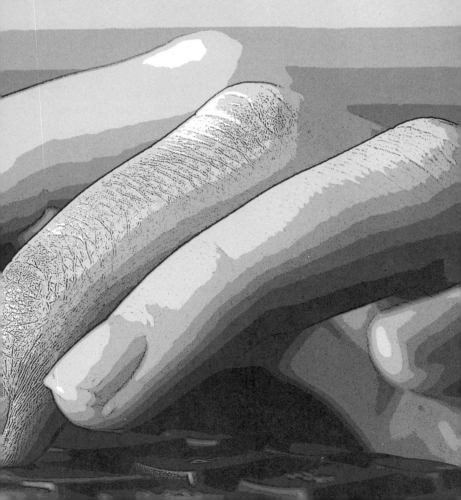

And that set the lot of them off, on one side or the other. Mamie grinned to herself. She and sam12 were like a team, but a team nobody knew about. It gave her a small thrill to feel he was saying things for her benefit, trying to impress her, making little in-jokes now that only she would understand. It felt good, it felt fun, it felt flattering.

And until the message popped into her inbox, it felt private.

>**Hey mamie_blues, r u and sam12 an item or what** ☺ ☺

Mamie stared at the message for a moment. TotallyTess: a bit of a know-all, a bit of a mother hen. Bossy, in other words, despite the two smileys. This called for some reticence.

>**What u mean??**

>**U and sam12 been talking among urselves??! What he just said!!**

Frowning, Mamie scrolled back. Oh,

right. Sam12 had forgotten the exchange about DVDs had been strictly between them. He'd made some reference to her watching Avatar tonight.

>**Talked 2 him about lucas_fan is all**
>**LOL, something u couldn't say on forum?!**

>**Yes**

Mamie drummed her fingernails on the edge of her laptop, waiting for TotallyTess's response.

>**OK hon, u be careful is all!** ☺

Oh for heaven's sake. Mamie was cross enough to type: >**What u mean?**

>**Just he's like all over u like a rash**

Deep breath. >**Don't think so. Hes just a pal. U jealous?!** She made a face. But she didn't want to fall out with TotallyTess, who could be sharp-tongued, or sharp-fingered or whatever. Better add a smiley to take out the sting.

>☺

The comeback was instant. >**Jealous, ha ha not really since he used to try it on with me!** ☺

As if. TotallyTess was a mother of two; she'd let that out during a discussion on kids' films. Hardly sam12's type. Mamie smirked. >**He's just a nice guy, don't read 2 much into it**

>**U know he used to think I was younger?**

Mamie made no comment, just sat back and waited.

>**Tried to ask where I lived**

Oh, for crying out loud. Not only was TotallyTess vain, she was paranoid. And way too old for sam12.

>**Yes well not like that with me so don't worry**

>**OK Im just saying. Anyway i always think its more sociable staying in the main**

chat room

Well, that was definitely an implied criticism, and not very subtly implied either. Mamie decided to ignore that last message, and instead swan regally back to the main discussion. Where she would make a point of stiletto-ing TotallyTess at the first opportunity.

Sam12 would like it, anyway.

Chapter Four

Mamie felt bleary the next day, sloping into school with a brain that felt like it was wrapped in cotton wool. Too much showing off in FilmFever, she was aware of that. If TotallyTess hadn't annoyed her so much, and if sam12 hadn't goaded her on, she might have got down to the *Romeo and Juliet* report a lot sooner, instead of scrawling the last ill-thought-out words at two in the morning.

And of course she hadn't had time to

watch a film. Fine, since her mother was hogging the TV anyway. She could have watched the DVD on her laptop, but she hadn't had time. Anyway, the chat room had been more fun.

She and sam12 just understood each other, simple as that. Same sense of humour. Of course she enjoyed his virtual company, who wouldn't?

Well, TotallyTess, for one. But she had no taste anyway.

Handing her report to Mr Mulgan, she felt a vague twinge of guilt. She knew it was not up to standard and she knew she was letting him down. But once in a school year wasn't so bad. She'd make it up to him with the next project, get back in his good books. Less easy to placate would be Nicky, who was being downright frosty this morning.

Rain was sheeting down the plate glass windows, and no one was venturing outside.

In a way that was lucky, since it meant she could corner Nicky. She was standing chatting to Martine and Becca, who each gave Mamie a chilly glance. Mamie pushed brashly into their gossiping group.

'Hi, Nicks. Did you get jeans?'

Nicky, looking rather as if she had a steel rod rammed down her spine, shook her head and opened her mouth to reply, but Becca beat her to it.

'We found this absolutely brilliant skirt, so we got that instead. Didn't we, Nicky?'

We, thought Mamie, half amused and half cheesed off. She ignored Becca.

'Really sorry I couldn't come, but I got the report finished.'

'Yeah? Good. So you'll be able to come out after school, then?'

It was a peace offering, but it was also a challenge. She'd agreed to be in FilmFever by four, for a discussion about eighties

slasher movies, but no way could she upset
Nicky twice, even she knew that. Mamie
forced a grin.

'Yeah, that would be brilliant.'

'Good.' Nicky brightened. 'It's late-
night shopping, remember? So we're going
to the mall for a pizza. Want to call your
mum?'

God, eating as well. She was going to
be *really* late and she hoped sam12 wouldn't
feel let down. 'That sounds good,' she lied.

The bell for the end of break drowned
out whatever Nicky said next. As it echoed
and she shook her head crossly, she said,
'You got Chemistry now? I'll walk you.'

Mamie fell into step beside her. No, it
really would be good to hang out with Nicky
for a while. Glancing at the rain dashing
against the windows, she sighed. 'Shame we
couldn't get outside just now. It's stuffy in
here.'

'Didn't think that would bother you. You're holed up in your room like a little mole most of the time anyway.'

'That's not true—'

'Oh, sorry.' Nicky gave her a sickly grin. 'Shouldn't nag. Despite your Vitamin D deficiency. For all I know you're a secret vampire.'

Mamie dug her in the ribs, glad their relationship was back on nagging and teasing terms. 'I am.'

'Could be a secret boyfriend, of course.'

'Nah...'

Nicky came to a halt and peered at her more closely. '*That* wasn't very convincing. Hang on, *is* there a boy?'

'No way!' Mamie laughed too loudly, then grinned and shrugged. 'OK, not a real one anyway.'

'No kidding!' Nicky's eyes lit with

curiosity. 'What, you've got an online boyfriend?'

Mamie blushed. 'No! Well, not really. Just a guy I like.'

'Ew! Has he got geeky specs and a Marvel comic habit?'

'Oi!' Mamie poked her in the ribs again.

'Well, have you seen his picture, or does he put up a photo of Edward Cullen?'

Mamie giggled. 'I dunno what he looks like.'

'You're kidding me. He might be a complete barfbag!'

'Jealous cow, you are.'

'Bet we could get him to email a photo. Eh? Whaddaya think, Mames?'

That was not a bad idea. Alone she might not have the nerve to ask, but with Nicky to back her up... 'OK. We'll give it a try.'

'Yeah! I'll be round your house tomorrow after school.'

'Tomorrow...'

'Tomorrow. You're not getting off shopping today. I mean, why would you *want* to?'

Chapter Five

>Hey mamie_blues what happened to u last night???

>Soz, sam12! Got held up, chat was finished by time I got in ☹

>No worries, were doin it again on Saturday, so how was school today ☺

Mamie stood up to let Nicky sit down to take a closer look.

'Well, his *typing* is perfectly presentable.' Nicky wrinkled her nose. 'But probably a barfbag, I'm telling you.'

'Not that I care what he looks like.'

'Yes, you do.' Nicky nudged her. 'Ask him, go on! Use me as an excuse if you have to!'

Mamie ignored her and leant over to type **>School was OK. How was the movie night b4 last?**

>Gr8. Really. You have to see that. How about the book report? U get it done?

'Hey, I thought you were talking movies all the time?' said Nicky.

'Yeah, yeah, in the chat room. We're not in there all the time. We can talk to each other as well.'

'I wanna see the chat room,' said Nicky in a mock-childish whine. 'And I wanna see *him*.'

>U there mamie?

Hurriedly she said **>Yep, just talking. Got report done**

>Talking 2 who?

>My mate Nicks. Mamie stood back;

then changing her mind she typed cheekily:

>**she wants to see what u look like, thinks u must be cute!** ☺ ☺ ☺

The cursor flickered at the side of the screen, but no words appeared. Sitting back, Mamie picked up her coffee and took a swig of it to kill the time. She felt a twinge of unease. Nicky peered closer to the screen.

'Has he gone?'

'Um... dunno.' Mamie clicked back to the main chat. They were talking about *Pulp Fiction*, one of sam12's favourites, but there was no sign of sam12 himself. No comment for at least a minute...

Five minutes later, there was still no sign of him. Paying attention with only half her brain to Nicky's chatter, Mamie dashed out a few curt sentences making comparisons and contrasts with *Kill Bill* – that had got him going in the past – but sam12 said not a word, and she withdrew swiftly from the discussion.

Nicky gave the screen an idle glance. 'You finished? Where's the boyfriend?'

'He's not a boyfriend,' Mamie retorted. 'He's just a pal.'

'What am I, processed cheese? Come on, let's go down the park and see if the boys are there.'

What boys? Mamie wanted to snap, but she knew perfectly well which ones. It would be Tyler and Rob and Calum and that crowd, and she'd be bored out of her skull. She had nothing in common with them. They wouldn't know Jackie Chan from Charlie Chan, because all they could talk about was football. To tell the truth, she'd be much the same with Ronaldo and Ronaldinho.

Still, it'd be an idea to get out of the house. She had a bad feeling about the way sam12 had just disappeared. He never did that. As a matter of fact, she couldn't think of a time when he hadn't replied to something she'd asked. Was he annoyed with her for that flirty remark? She'd only been repeating what Nicky said, for heaven's sake. Why so sensitive?

Still, FilmFever didn't hold quite the same attraction without him, and for once she was almost relieved to leave the chat room and walk down to the park. She was subdued, but Nicky didn't seem to mind that, covering her silence with raucous giggles and inane chatter with the boys. She seemed happy just to have got Mamie to herself, outside and miles from the distractions of her laptop. Mamie leaned against the swing frame, half-listening to Nicky, running and re-running the online conversation in her head while she resisted Tyler's advances with no trouble at all.

The stupid exchange was still buzzing through her brain at two in the morning, and by that time she was certain she'd blown it. Staring at a patch of reflected street light on the ceiling, her head fuzzy with sleeplessness, she felt a small twinge of relief.

He was a friend. If he fancied her, it wasn't in the way Tyler did, with all those clumsy innuendoes and over-eager jokes. She was pretty sure she hadn't misread sam12's signals. She had reacted badly, that was all. And as miserable as that was making her right now, it was also kind of reassuring.

He wasn't out to hit on her. He'd actually, genuinely liked her. He hadn't just been faking it when he admired the extent of her knowledge or the sharpness of her observations. He did actually like her and respect her opinions.

And that was kind of nice.

Mamie rolled over, hauling on the duvet, trying to pummel the pillow into comfy submission. It was no good, her muscles were tied up in knots as much as her brain. She wasn't going to get any sleep like this.

Hauling her duvet round her – the heating wasn't on at this hour – she crept silently past her mother's door, holding her breath and pausing to listen for the deep breathing that verged on snores. Great, she was well out of it, it was unlikely she'd hear the TV. Closing the lounge door carefully, Mamie hunted through the DVDs and pulled out something undemanding... a mild romcom, that would do. Curling onto the sofa and tugging the duvet round her, she clicked the remote with one exposed finger and waited for the slightly boring plot to send her to sleep.

It wasn't working. Restlessly she clicked across to a TV channel, then surfed them all for films: two horror movies, an ancient western, an achingly slow Japanese art-house movie and a fairly recent thriller. She couldn't concentrate on any of them, because they were all going straight over the top of her head. She wasn't thinking about these people and their life traumas.

She was thinking about sam12.

Clicking the TV off, she sneaked back to her bedroom and opened up the chat room on her laptop screen. If she DM'd him now, she might get to sleep and she

wouldn't be too nervous to do it in the morning. Play innocent, she thought, fingers hovering over the keyboard...

>**Hi sam12, cant sleep so just seeing if ur around. Wonder what happd earlier, u had computer probs?**

There. If he didn't message her back in the morning, he was definitely hacked off. At least she'd contacted him. She knew she'd never summon up the nerve if she waited till morning.

Be interesting to see if anyone was in the chat room, though, and it might make her feel sleepy. Sure enough, a discussion was going on about *Chicago* and *Moulin Rouge!* and their respective merits. Not a very lively discussion, since they were all breathless fans of both. Some of them were obviously on the other side of the world. Well, they would be at this hour.

She almost jumped when the direct

message notification popped up.

>**Hey mamie, ur awake late. U got ur friend there?**

>**No. Ur up late too!!!**

>**Yeh**

It wasn't like him to be so unforthcoming. She waited almost a minute, but nothing more. Biting her lip, she typed

>**Ur quiet, u annoyed with me?**

>**Nah its OK**

>**Er yeh, something wrong i think...**

>**Honest its fine. Just wasn't expecting ur friend earlier**

>**Did u mind?**

>**Well I kind of always think DMing is private. U know what I mean? Not like the chat room**

>**C what u mean. Sorry if u were upset**

>**No, not upset honest. Just surprised. Just kind of always imagine Im just**

talking to u. Bit of a shock if somebody else is listening, u know?

Sam12 had a point, she had to admit. And once again, it was nice to know he was as concerned about his privacy as she was. That had to be good. A little ashamed about inflicting Nicky on him, she hesitated, unsure what to say. Luckily he must have known she was feeling awkward, because he stepped in.

>So what are u doing @ the weekend?

>Goin out with friends, she typed back, swamped with relief. He'd forgiven her.

>Cool. Not ur weekend to c ur dad then?

>No, thats next weekend. Really looking forward to seeing him

>Oh thats really nice ☺ U said he was near here, didn't u?

Mamie waited, twisting her fingers together, but there was no sign of him making the suggestion she wanted. So what now?

Was he going to think she was stupid, or flirty, or just plain brash? But his objection to Nicky hadn't been the cheeky remark, just that she was kind of invading their privacy, and Mamie had encouraged her. That was fair enough.

Sam12 seemed reticent – and that was *good* – but he was the one who'd brought up the subject of her dad. Which had to mean something, after all. He was just shy of making the next obvious suggestion, scared how it would look.

Mamie took a breath.

>**I'm going on the train. Goes thru Edgerton, u don't want 2 meet for coffee do u?**

She shut her eyes, almost afraid to see his response. Maybe there wouldn't be one. Maybe he'd go back to the chat room and never DM her again. Maybe she'd blown it. Oh well. It was done now. She peered nervously at the screen.

>Srsly?? That wd b gr8!! U sure it
won't make u late?

>Its an open tckt, can use it anytime.
Can just let dad know when 2 expect me.
An hr late wont matter

>That wd be fantastic, really. But ur
sure u don't mind being late 4 ur dad?

>Srsly, no worries. I'll leave mums at usual time, get off @ Edgerton, take the next train an hr later. Wd be fun to meet up! ☺

>Be gr8! Looking fwd to it already
>Is there station cafe? That wd work

Hesitation as the cursor blinked.

>**Station caff's not v nice,** he typed.
>**Tell u what, I'll meet u at Breadbasket. Nice little cafe, easy 2 get 2. Turn left out of station, right into 1st lane, u cant miss it. What time?**

It was going to work. Mamie felt ridiculously excited now. Sam12 might be incredibly boring in real life, or have irredeemable acne or something, but he was unlikely to agree to a meeting if that was true. And she wanted to know. They had a real friendship, a real connection, so much in common. She didn't know anyone at school who understood her like sam12 did.

And if it didn't work out, so what? It was a bit of fun, just a matter of meeting a virtual friend and making him into a real one. Never mind that the little tug in her gut felt a lot like romantic excitement...

And if she was spending less and less time in the chat room, and more and more

time in private little meetings with sam12, so what? He was the most interesting person there. He listened to her, which was more than could be said for some of them, especially TotallyTess, who was incredibly snotty lately.

They'd get back to FilmFever. And she and sam12 were a team now, a proper team. Wait till the jealous TotallyTess realised that...

She must be feeling guilty though. She realised that from the way she was so impatient with Nicky, the way she couldn't concentrate at school, even on subjects she liked, the way she snapped at her mother and got her head bitten off in return.

It would do them both good to have a break for a weekend. Mamie was really looking forward to it; mostly because of her dad, of course. Mostly...

Though she did feel guilty about lying to him.

Thing was, there was no point telling her father or her mother the truth. They'd only forbid it. They would think it was something sinister, rather than an innocent meeting with a mate. And much as they argued and fought with each other, on some issues her parents could be terrifyingly united.

Chapter Six

Sam12 wasn't kidding about the station cafe.
Mamie wrinkled her nose as she squeezed
her backpack through the ticket barrier.
Across the concourse, next to a WH Smith
that seemed to be the only shop, she could
see the cafe's dirty glass panes and the rickety
pine tables inside. The people sitting there
were still wrapped up in their coats and
scarves so it must be as cold in there as it was
out here, where a stiff wind funnelled down
the tracks and cut right through her skin.

Mamie glanced at her watch. She had an hour till the next train came through, but it would go quickly. She'd better start looking for the Breadbasket. Now that she was here, now that she'd actually taken the decision to get off the train at Edgerton, she was a lot more nervous than she'd expected.

Still, she'd better go through with it now she was here. Hitching her backpack onto one shoulder, she followed the thin crowds to the station exit. *Turn left*, he'd said. That was where most people were heading, so it wasn't difficult. And *first lane on the right*.

She paused at the corner. It was a narrow cobbled alley, but without much charm, not in this weather anyway. There were boutiques, though, and an expensive-looking restaurant, and pretty wrought-iron streetlights that were obviously a well-maintained feature. Perfectly respectable.

The Breadbasket was a cosy-looking place, down a couple of steps and warmly lit. As Mamie opened the door a bell rang, and she felt suddenly self-conscious as faces turned to her. But they turned just as quickly back to their pancakes and jam, or whatever. She scanned the room quickly, then sat down in a quiet corner, wishing the shadows could swallow her up. There were two mothers with pushchairs and grizzling toddlers, three old ladies at the centre table, and a man in a leather jacket sitting by himself. No sign of sam12. Yet, she told herself firmly.

Oh, this was mad. He wasn't going to show up. She was wasting time and money too, because she was going to have to buy at least a cup of coffee, and by the look of the menu her cheapest option was a carafe of something Kenyan. She ordered it from the waitress, shook her head at the offer of something to eat, and sat back, determined to drink the coffee as fast as she could and go back to the station. She might even call her father, confess to her silly plan and get him to pick her up here.

She rummaged in the side pocket of her backpack, pulled out her phone and flicked it open, staring at his number.

Or maybe not...

Nah. Mamie shoved the phone back into the backpack pocket. She concentrated on pushing down the plunger on the carafe without sending the coffee spurting everywhere. She did it slowly, to kill time, so she wasn't aware of the figure who stood up and moved across to her table – not till he was standing over her, smiling.

Glancing up, she let herself smile back. It was the man in the leather jacket. He was good-looking, brown-haired, quite stocky with a pleasant face and sparky dark brown eyes.

'Hi!' he said.

'Hi...'

'You're Mamie, right?'

She felt her shoulders slump with relief. 'Hi! You know Sam, right? Has he been held up?'

The man pulled out a chair and sat down opposite her. 'Um. Well, I *am* Sam.'

Mamie could only stare at him. 'Sam12?'

'The very same! Hey, is something wrong?'

He was so open, so friendly and so obviously delighted to see her that she felt quite embarrassed. 'No, nothing's wrong. It's nice to meet you. At last!' She made herself grin, and a nervous laugh escaped.

It couldn't be. It couldn't be sam12. This guy had to be in his early thirties, maybe? Thirty at the youngest.

'Here, you want something to eat? Go on, don't make me feel like a pig. The scones are great.'

It filled the awkward silence, anyway. It was something to do with her hands while she let her confused mind get itself back in gear. So this was sam12. Had she misread something? She had to give herself a moment to think, and anyway he seemed perfectly nice. A bit older than she'd expected, sure, but he was as natural and friendly as he was in the chat room.

'Here.' He pushed the miniature jars of jam across to her, and she busied herself spreading some on a scone. 'How was the train?'

She managed to smile. 'The train was fine. So were you waiting in here long?'

'I got here ten minutes early. Didn't want to be late.' He smiled again.

Mamie glanced at her watch, then felt guilty, because he must have noticed the gesture. Oh relax, she told herself crossly. She made herself drop her shoulders and smile more naturally at him, and tried to ease herself a little more into the conversation.

So he wasn't the schoolboy she'd expected: so what? He was a perfectly nice guy and she'd arranged to meet him, so she might as well be polite. He could still be a friend. That was all she'd wanted, after all. A friend, someone to talk to, someone who understood her obsessions and could laugh about the same things. Just because he wasn't the same age didn't mean she had to cut him dead now. Besides, he had nice kind

eyes, and a catchy smile.

'Can I ask you something?' he said as she laughed at one of his jokes and drank more coffee.

'Uh-huh. Go ahead.'

'Well, Mamie...' Sam blushed, and then let the words come out in a rush. 'How old are you, Mamie?'

She eyed him. 'Did I not tell you on the forum? I'm fourteen. Or will be next month.'

His eyes widened. 'Thirteen? You're kidding! You look a *lot* older.'

'I thought I told you how old I was...'

'No, you never did.' He smiled. 'You come across as so sophisticated, so knowledgeable. Maybe that's why I was confused.'

But I'm pretty sure I did tell you, thought Mamie. 'I kind of thought you were younger. I mean, you talked about homework.'

'I don't think so. Oh, I might have mentioned essays. Was that it? I'm a student.'

She studied him sceptically. He looked a bit too old even for that.

'I mean, a correspondence course,' he added. 'Open University. I missed university first time round, so I'm catching up. Here, you want another coffee?'

Nervously she checked her watch. 'I'm not sure. I...'

'Don't worry about the train. If we're late I can run you to your dad's. You said he was in Cheddingham, right? It's only fifteen miles down the road.'

'Well. I'll try and get the train, there's still time.' Mamie shrugged, tempted. 'But go on, then, I'll have another coffee. What was that you were saying about Tobey Maguire?'

'Well, not so much him as Sam Raimi...'

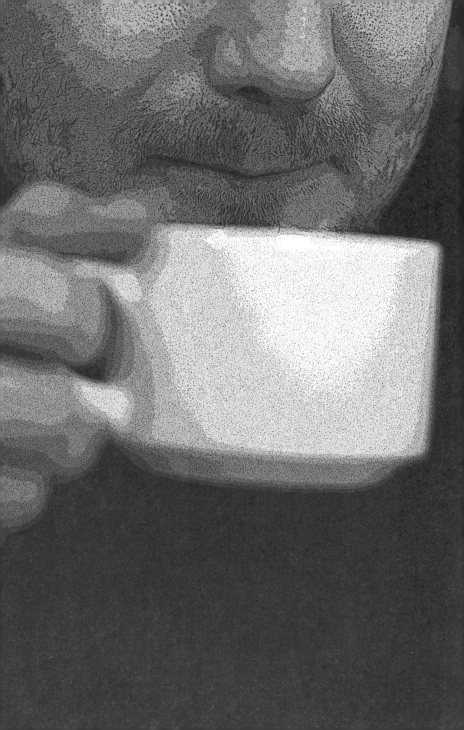

He leaned forward eagerly and went on expounding his thesis.

He was smart, and entertaining too. Despite her laughter, though, Mamie found her mind wandering. Sam Raimi. That reminded her. 'I used to wonder if that was how you chose your name,' she said as he paused to take a swig of his coffee.

'Huh?'

'You know, sam12, from Sam Raimi. Because you went on about the Spider Man movies so much when I was first in the chat room.' She grinned at him. 'But it's nice that you use your real name.'

'Oh, yeah.' He set his cup down. 'Right! And of course, plain "Sam" was taken.'

'But listen, what about the third film? What did you think?'

They both had plenty to say on the subject, and when Sam finally glanced at his own watch, he stood up very suddenly and pushed back his chair. 'Oh no. Come on, you might just make it.'

Checking her own watch, she doubted it. Breathlessly Mamie grabbed her backpack, swearing under her breath. But she didn't feel as panicked as she might have. He'd offered a lift, after all. She wondered if that had been in the back of her mind all the time, actually. He was such good

company, and she didn't want to go just yet, and it would be a lot better than getting back on a train. And she hadn't expected sam12 to have a car, after all, and it was kind of a nice surprise that he did.

Sam picked up the bill and left it on the table with some cash on top of it and a coin tip. They were out of the door before the waitress had time to ring it through, and

then Sam had taken her hand and they were running for the station. She wasn't altogether happy with that – it felt funny to be hand in hand with a bloke who wasn't her father – but he did seem to be getting her through the crowds faster. They skidded to a halt on the platform, just in time to watch the 3.40 pull away and pick up speed.

'Oh, no,' moaned Mamie. 'I'll have to phone Dad.'

'No, you won't.' Sam hadn't let go of her hand, she noticed. 'Come on, I can get you there in 20 minutes. No slower than the train. Seriously, I wasn't kidding. And it's my fault, I held you up.'

'Sure...?' Mamie eased her hand out of his, and as if he'd only just realised what he was doing, he quickly let it go with an apologetic smile. She was being silly, getting uneasy over the least little thing.

'Honestly. I don't have to work this

afternoon. And I feel like I owe you, sorry.'

'OK then.' She smiled.

Walking at his side – no hand-holding, she thought with relief – she wasn't sorry she'd missed the train. This wasn't something she was going to make a habit of, but he was fun, and good company, and perfectly polite. She doubted she'd make an effort to meet him again, though. She realised that for all her inward protestations, she'd been feeling romantically drawn to sam12, and that clearly wasn't an option.

He'd turned a couple of corners before he pulled the car keys from his pocket. The light and locks bleeped on a smart dark Toyota. Mamie raised her eyebrows as he opened the door. It had an almost-new number plate.

'Nice car,' she said admiringly.

'Thanks. I only got it a couple of months ago.' He took her backpack firmly

from her hands and slung it into the back
seat, then looked up at her expectantly as he
got into the driver's seat.

She hesitated. Silly to be anxious now.
She just hadn't expected him to have such
an expensive and obviously new car.
Somehow it reinforced how old he was. She
definitely wasn't doing this again. Maybe she
shouldn't do it now. Mamie bit her lip,

thinking about her phone in the backpack pocket.

'Better go, you'll be late!'

If the phone had been in her jeans pocket, she'd just have pulled it out and phoned her dad. *No worries,* she'd have said. *Look, I really don't want to put you to so much trouble. I'll call my dad.* And she'd have pushed the speed dial button before Sam could object.

But the phone was in the backpack. It would be way too embarrassing to open the back door and rummage for it. Actually, it'd be downright rude.

Shrugging, more to herself than to him, Mamie got into the front seat. Never again, that was all.

'Don't forget your seat belt,' he smiled.

Chapter Seven

Sam seemed a lot quieter as he drove, which wasn't exactly reassuring. A couple of times Mamie tried to start a conversation, but he looked so distracted by the rain and by driving, she gave up after a while.

'Sorry.' He gave her a sidelong smile. 'I'm just concentrating on the road. The system going out of town, it's murder.'

Nice expression, thought Mamie with an inward shiver.

She could see his point, though. The

lanes and the signs as they drove up onto a busy bypass were incredibly confusing; or that was how they seemed to her. Sam had to brake quite suddenly for an exit, and shift lanes quickly, getting a flash from the driver he cut up.

'Nearly missed that one,' he said.

Mamie glanced at him, noticing sweat beaded along his hairline. 'Thought you'd know it pretty well. How long've you lived here?'

'Oh, they keep changing the priorities,' he muttered, flicking on his indicator and changing lanes again into a slip road.

Take the chance, Mamie told herself. Touching his arm to get his attention, she felt him jump, and pulled her hand away quickly. 'Listen, I feel really bad about this. See there, there's a lay-by?' She pointed at the sign indicating it was coming up. 'If you pull in there I'll just call Dad. He won't mind, honest. I didn't realise it was going to be this awkward. I'm really sorry.'

'No. It's OK. We're nearly out of town. Then it's fine.'

Mamie shifted in her seat, looking longingly at the lay-by as it swept past them. 'I guess Dad could meet us halfway. If I call him now—'

Turning awkwardly, she stretched to reach her backpack, but strong fingers closed on her arm and pulled her back into her seat. The suddenness and the roughness were shocking, and for a moment, as she sat back blinking, she didn't know what to think.

Then a bolt of real fear zinged through her gut.

'Sorry, um—' Sam looked very nervous now. 'Sorry. But there's no need to phone your dad, we're nearly there.'

Mamie leaned forward, suddenly unwilling to stay in her seat like a good girl.

Her fingers were trembling as they strayed hesitantly to her seatbelt plug. 'I don't really, um... I don't recognise this road?'

'Yes, well.' Sam scratched the side of his face. 'This is kind of the pretty way. I just wanted to show you where I live.'

'I thought you lived in Edgerton.'

'Near Edgerton, I think I said.'

'I don't think you... How near Edgerton?'

'Well, just up this way a bit.'

Mamie looked at her watch. 20 minutes, he'd said. She'd been in this car for 40 already. And they looked no closer to Cheddingham. Her heart began to thunder, so loud and hard she thought Sam must be able to hear it.

It wasn't as if her father had lived in Cheddingham for long. He'd only moved out a year ago. So she'd been here maybe ten times? All the same, she'd thought she would recognise the surrounding countryside well enough. But maybe the train went a different way, that was all...

No. Not this different. And she couldn't even put it down to the dismal weather. The fields here were flatter, and they'd just passed a big sprawling quarry that she'd never seen before. It was just more desolate, somehow, than the gentle green fields approaching Cheddingham, with patches of woodland and trickling streams giving way to pretty suburbs and a slightly soulless town centre. The fields on either side of Sam's car had an unkempt look, and she caught sight of a railway line that looked overgrown and disused.

'Sam?'

He was frowning, concentrating on the road.

'Sam?'

'Uh. Yeah?'

'Is it your real name? Sam.'

'Course it is.'

She knew, from the way he wouldn't look at her, that it wasn't. She stayed silent, watching the dreary countryside unfold. No sign of a town.

'Well, look, it's not really,' he said at last. 'They say you shouldn't, don't they?'

Mamie nodded.

'It's not *sinister*. It's just – I don't like people knowing my real name online. I mean, look at what you did!'

He sounded almost aggressive now, angry with her. In a small voice she said, 'What?'

'Well, there was you letting that friend of yours see private messages. It just shows, you can never tell what's happening when you're online. I was really annoyed about that.'

Mamie nodded. Yes, she remembered.

She thought maybe she should say, 'And there was you lying to me about your age and your name,' but she knew it wouldn't be a good idea to get into an argument. 'I know, I'm really sorry about that...'

'I hope so. I mean, private messages are private messages, aren't they? I don't like saying things when I don't know who's listening. I nearly didn't contact you again. I nearly left the whole chat room because of that.'

Mamie was beginning to wish he had.

'But we're OK now. Don't worry about it. I mean, I don't blame you. You just didn't know. We're still friends now, aren't we?'

'Yes.'

Her whole body was rigid. She didn't dare glance at her watch, but when she looked at the car's digital clock she knew they'd been driving for an hour now. And they weren't anywhere near Cheddingham.

'Where are we going?'

'Well, I thought – you know, I thought I could just show you around on the way. Show you where I live, sort of thing.'

'I thought you lived near Edgerton.' She couldn't keep the tremor out of her voice.

'Well, not *that* near.' He gave a short breathy laugh, as if the misunderstanding was a bit funny. But it didn't sound genuine.

'You knew that café—'

'Oh yeah, I just googled it. There was a map. It was nice, wasn't it? Glad I found it.'

Googled it. Found a map.

There wasn't any point getting into an argument, she told herself again. No point at all. All she knew was that she had to get out of this car. But not only was he driving at a steady pace, fast if inside the speed limit, the countryside was still desolate, with only occasional dreary houses that she gazed at with hopeless longing as they passed into the distance. And the sky was darkening. It was no longer afternoon, it was a deepening evening.

'Tell you what,' she said, forcing brightness into her voice. 'I'll just get out here. I can call my dad and he'll pick me up.'

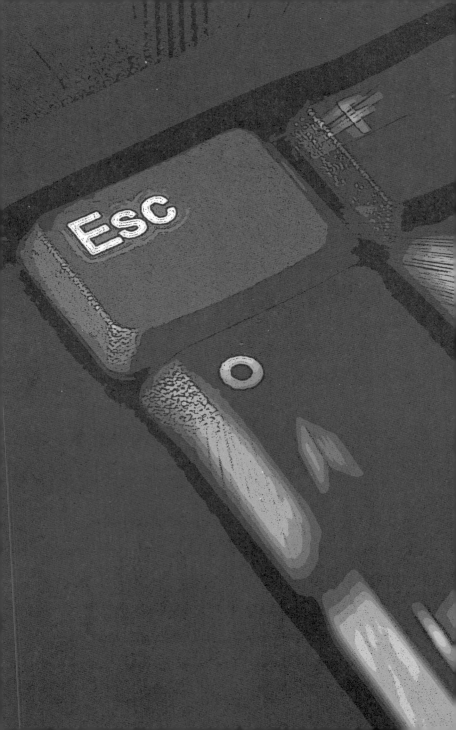

'Don't be silly.' Sam didn't look at her. 'We don't want to put him to all that trouble. It's quite a way back from here. I'll take you back afterwards.'

'Afterwards,' repeated Mamie, but barely any sound came out.

'After I've shown you my place,' he said. There was a hint of irritation in his voice now.

OK, so the quiet and timid attitude wasn't working. 'I really want you to stop and let me out now.' That wasn't so bad. She sounded quite firm and assertive, considering her whole body felt chilled and her heart wouldn't stop thrashing. 'I'll call my dad, it's fine. But I want to get out and go home now. I don't want to come and see your place. If you pull over right here...' She reached again for her backpack, more determinedly this time.

He braked, but only enough to grab

her arm and pull her back into her seat. This time he didn't apologise. 'You've got a nerve!' he snapped.

'I have?' She was angry and scared enough to snap back.

'You girls. Changing your minds when you feel like it.'

Girls. Minds. She didn't like the sound of this. 'I don't know what you mean.'

'Leading us on, coming over all friendly and chatty and *flirty.* And then suddenly you think you can say, "Oh I want to go home, I want my daddy," and we're expected to just drop everything and give you a lift halfway across the county? It's so *selfish.*'

'Who's us?' she asked, trembling again. Surreptitiously she tried the door handle, but it was centrally locked.

'Men, you know. You're just like this with us all. I bet your mum led your dad on all the time. And then she dumped him, right?'

'No, she didn't. They didn't get on so they agreed to split up...'

'I bet she's a bitch to him. I bet she's always asking him for money.'

'She asks him for money but he's happy to give it to her. They're still friendly. Most of the time.'

'Yeah, I bet. She's friendly when she needs his money. You're the one who said she didn't like him watching films all the time.'

Oh God, yeah. She remembered that. She'd just been chatting, making conversation, being funny. Moaning a bit about her parents but not seriously. 'They didn't get on, I told you. It doesn't mean they hate each other.'

He wasn't listening. 'Yeah, she's got what she wants out of him, so she dumps him. That's what you do, isn't it? And now you think you can do the same to me. Like mother, like daughter, right?'

'But I didn't–'

'You come on all friendly in the chat room; what am I supposed to think? You can't deny you were flirting with me.'

I wasn't, thought Mamie desperately. I did flirt a bit, it's true, and I wish I hadn't. But I flirted with sam12; I flirted with a fifteen-year-old boy, not with you. Whoever you are...

'You're the one who suggested meeting up!' he almost shouted. 'You!'

Oh, God.

'Look, I don't want us to fall out.' He reached across to pat her knee. 'Let's not argue, OK? It was a misunderstanding, that's all.' He was smiling again, and it creeped her out even more than his moments of unpredictable aggression.

All she wanted to do was find the

central lock and throw herself out of the car. She had to almost force herself down into the seat to stop herself, because what would be the point? She wouldn't be able to grab her backpack, so she would be without her phone, and how could she flag down a car before the fake Sam turned back for her?

She still didn't quite believe it. She wanted this to be a simple mistake. There *was* a sam12; she'd just left the Breadbasket with the wrong guy, and soon he'd realise his mistake too, and they'd go back. Was that why he was taking a sliproad onto a motorway in the gathering dark? Turning back? But no, they were merging into the northbound carriageway...

Maybe she was misinterpreting all his remarks: there was nothing sinister about him, there *couldn't* be, because this couldn't be happening. She was paranoid. She'd been watching way too many gruesome thrillers. There was a perfectly logical explanation for all of this. Even sam12 was turning into an almost-real presence in her head: the boy she should have met, the boy she'd known online. It was next to impossible to believe he didn't exist.

Mamie stared through the windscreen, trying to think. She had to start believing, because this was trouble, real trouble, and she was in it. There was no misunderstanding. She knew that from his sickly smile, from his quick temper, from the way he'd patted her knee and left his hand there to squeeze it.

Physically she couldn't match him. There was no point thinking of jumping out and making a run for it. Panic squeezed her chest again, and she had to take deep breaths, as quietly as she could. She had to look calm. Like this was normal. Like she was perfectly happy with the situation.

'So long as you don't get into trouble. I don't want you to get into any trouble.'

He gave her a quizzical look. 'Why would I get in trouble?'

'Well, you know how they are about the underage thing. You know. Schoolgirls having, like romances–' she had to choke out the word '–with older guys.'

'That's not a problem. I mean, you wouldn't tell, would you?'

'Course not.'

'Because you know how angry I was about your friend seeing our private messages. I mean, it would be awful if anybody else did.'

'Yes. Don't worry. Although...' She bit her lip. 'They can find things on your computer, can't they? They can go back and find stuff, even if you delete it.'

His face wrinkled in perplexity. 'Why would I have to delete anything? You asked me to meet you,' he said again. 'You're my girl, you're here because you want to be. With me.'

'Of course. It's just that people make such a fuss.'

'Anyway, I didn't use my own computer. I go to this cybercafe.' He hesitated. 'Well, a few cybercafes actually. Different ones.'

Her heart shrank inside her. 'In the middle of the night?'

'Oh no, that was the computer at work. Don't worry about that. Loads of people have access to it.'

Which didn't mean they wouldn't work it out, thought Mamie. It didn't mean they wouldn't track him down, whatever delusions he had. But by then it would be too late.

Funnily enough, the horrible thought didn't make her feel any worse. It almost made her colder and more determined. There wasn't any point panicking, after all.

There wasn't any point shivering with fear. And there was certainly no point asking him to let her out of the car.

'You're not still angry with me, are you?' She made herself look at him.

'Of course not! Why would I be? It isn't your fault.'

Maybe, she thought, maybe if he got what he wanted he'd let her go. It would be terrible, horrific, but she'd be OK. In the end. She'd be alive. He actually believed she fancied him. He thought she was his girlfriend. So he wouldn't actually hurt her or anything...

'Is it much further?'

'Not far.'

She waited for him to explain, but it seemed it was all he was willing to say.

'Only, I really need to go to the loo.'

'That's OK. You can go later. We'd better press on.'

She jiggled in her seat, smiled ruefully at him. 'I mean I really, *really* need to go, Sam.'

She had to make herself say his false name, and then she wondered if she should have bothered. He looked a bit suspicious, as if she was trying too hard.

Reaching across, she laid her hand on his thigh, trying not to snatch it instantly away; trying not to gag as she patted it affectionately.

'S'OK. I'll last. Don't worry.' She squirmed again, and that made her hand jiggle too. Now she couldn't bear it any longer, but she made herself draw it away quite slowly and fold both hands demurely in her lap.

'You're a nice girl. Know that?'

'Oh, that's sweet!' She giggled a bit. 'You're a nice guy, too.'

God's sake, Mamie, she told herself.

Don't lay it on too thick.

He didn't seem to mind, though. 'I've never met anyone like you, Mamie. You're not like those other girls. You're really... genuine. Honest. For real.'

'I hope so. Not sure my parents would agree!'

'Well, parents don't always understand, do they? They don't understand you're your own person. Can make your own decisions. You know?'

'That's right,' she agreed. 'I mean, I'm a grown up, aren't I?'

'You certainly are.' He smiled again.

'Is it really much further?'

'Why?'

'Cos I really am desperate, and I'm worried about your new car.'

His nose wrinkled in slight distaste, and his foot eased off the accelerator. She sensed he really was torn. She'd bet he'd be the kind of guy who wouldn't want his car upholstery ruined. Not to mention the DNA she might leave... *no*. She wasn't going to think like that.

Again Mamie jiggled in her seat. 'I won't be a minute, honest. There's a services–' she glanced at the motorway sign in his headlights '–in five miles. Can we pull in there?'

'Tell you what.' He glanced in the mirror and slewed across to the inside lane, then flicked on his indicator again and pulled right onto the hard shoulder. 'No problem. Just go here.'

Mamie's whole body froze. 'Here?'

He pulled on the handbrake, left the engine running. 'Yes. Go on, I thought you were bursting. It's dark, nobody's going to see you.'

He leaned right across her to open the door. Instinctively she pressed back into the

car seat, desperate that he shouldn't touch her. Then she thought, don't be stupid, Mamie. He was already suspicious.

She touched his shoulder. 'Thanks. Really.' She clambered out into the cold yellow motorway light.

'Don't be long.'

'No.' She looked left and right. Since when were motorways so quiet? What was she going to *do*? Three cars swept by, and she wanted to cry, because she didn't have the courage to run out in front of them. 'It's a bit bright. I'm just going onto the verge a bit.'

'Not far. You might get lost.'

In my dreams, mate. 'No, not far.'

She stepped over the small steel barrier and into the long grass. The ground wasn't soft; there was gravel underfoot and the grass was sparse. She looked up and around, as if looking for a shadowy spot. The man who called himself Sam had opened his own door and started to get out, and panic swept through her in a cold wave.

'Don't watch, OK?'

He stared at her over the roof of the car. 'Hurry up, then.'

'I'll be two seconds.' She undid her belt and the top button of her jeans, and threw him a smile. He wouldn't know how sickly it was, not in this horrible amber light.

He chose to take it as she'd hoped: a flirtatious promise of *later*. Winking as he grinned back, he got back into the car seat.

Shut the door, she begged inwardly.

He didn't.

Crouching in the dark, she made herself pee. Slowly she stood up and refastened her jeans. He was watching her in the rear-view mirror, she just knew it. How was she going to move, even? Her muscles were stiff with terror.

Be in a movie, she thought. It's not real. Don't be Mamie. Be Kate Beckinsale, be Jennifer Garner, be... be Uma Thurman. *Don't be Mamie...*

Yanking her belt hard into its buckle, she glanced once back at the car and the man, waiting for her.

And then she bolted.

Such a small barrier, she should have jumped it easily, but her foot caught. Nerves, terror. She stumbled but she didn't fall; and then she was running into the motorway lanes.

He was out of the car, yelling at her, screaming her name, but all she could hear was the roar of traffic on the opposite carriageway. Much more going south than north. She kept running, faster than she'd ever run in her life, because she could hear him behind her, not ten metres back and gaining. Mamie sobbed in a breath. One car, two cars swept past, slowing but not stopping. A third, starting to stop, then changing his mind, shaking his head. She glanced at the barrier between the carriageways, wanting to leap it, scared of mistiming the jump again. Her breath sobbed in and out of her lungs, and she couldn't resist glancing back as a faster car swerved and blared its horn.

More cars slewed around her. She was going to cause a crash – but she had to get away before he came looking in his car...

A van had pulled up on the hard shoulder. Mamie didn't think she could go on running – didn't think she could go on *breathing* – so she had to decide. Bolting across to it, she flung herself at the man who got out to yell at her.

'What the–' he said, and swore.

She dodged behind him, shoving him in front of her even as he barked another curse, but there was no need. The man called Sam had turned on his heel, jogging back in the direction of his car, then suddenly putting on a burst of speed till he reached it.

She was crying, she realised. Sobbing for breath, but crying too.

'Please,' she managed to gasp through her tears. 'Please can you phone my dad?'

Chapter Eight

'You're a lucky girl,' said the police officer as she stood up to leave.

She was a family liaison officer. Apart from that, Mamie had no idea what rank she was. No idea. They all blended into each other and she couldn't think straight yet. She didn't think she wanted to think. Not in depth, and not for long. It had been that way for a month. If she started to think she'd have nightmares, she knew it, and the sleeping pills were keeping those at bay just now.

All the cops seemed to say, 'You're a lucky girl.' Maybe it was pre-programmed into their circuits. Unless you weren't lucky, of course. Mamie felt her father's hand tighten on hers, and her mother hugged her tightly. She felt almost suffocated by them, since they didn't seem to want to let go of her, but she was really OK with that.

'Those girls,' her mum kept saying. 'Those poor girls.'

It hadn't taken them long to track him down, not with his number plate on the motorway cameras. And they'd tracked his progress the whole way down to Edgerton, because of course he wasn't from anywhere remotely near Edgerton. He was from much further up in the north-west, from a little anonymous town, where he lived in a little anonymous house with a big fence and terrible secrets in its garden. Two terrible secrets.

'It might have been more,' said Mamie's father.

'Don't say that,' said her mother. 'Don't say that again.'

'Not just our Mamie,' he said. 'I don't mean that. He'd have gone on, wouldn't he? So there'd have been other girls. I think Mamie should remember that. She's probably saved other girls from him.'

Mamie would rather not have had to save anybody, but she didn't say anything. She pulled out her mobile instead and flipped it open. A message from Nicky.

'I'm going out,' she said. As gently as she could, she wriggled out of her mother's embrace and stood up before she could change her mind.

'Oh! Are you sure?' Her mother stood up too.

'Yeah. I'm going to meet Nicky.'

'You don't want me to come? Or Dad? Just to keep you company on the walk,' she added hurriedly.

'No. Really. I'm fine.' It wasn't just that she was stir crazy from being at home every evening, and bored, and antsy. It was her itchy fingers. Incredibly enough, she wanted to go back to FilmFever.

TotallyTess had emailed her. The chat room had closed down, but it had reopened under another name and with some of the same members, this time with a moderator. Like getting back on a horse after a hard fall, she had to go back there, talk to friends. Easygoing friends who didn't make demands or suggestions, who didn't want to know your name but didn't tell you a fake one either. Like TotallyTess, who'd tried to warn her. Who'd really been very nice to her in the email, considering.

Sam12 wasn't going to spoil her life

any more than he already had. And FilmFever would be safer now, safer than a lot of chat rooms.

Still, she wasn't quite ready...

Nicky was waiting on their favourite park bench, waving a can of Coke. 'Hello, you.'

'Hi.' Mamie sat down, hands in her pockets, then changed her mind and took the Coke.

'So how you doing?'

'Fine.' Not quite true. She still felt like she was living in a bubble. A very thin bubble, which was going to burst one day when she'd realise how close she'd come to dying. Mamie knew she couldn't face that knowledge, not right now. Right now she was trying her hardest to keep the bubble intact around her.

'Well.' Nicky sprawled back against the bench and closed her eyes. 'Suppose you'll be fine now, sure enough. I mean, you were the dipstick who arranged to meet him.'

'What?' Mamie drew back, stung to the heart. 'It wasn't my fau–'

'Almost totally your fault. *Dipstick*.'

Mamie jumped to her feet, violently hurt, ready to lash out verbally or even physically. Only then the bubble might break... Clenching her fists, she glared at Nicky, then slowly, carefully, sat down again.

'In a way... maybe...'

'But not mostly,' added Nicky in a nicer voice. 'But just daft. Not, like, evil.' Cheerfully she poked Mamie's ribs.

Oi. Watch my bubble. Mamie suddenly felt more miserable than anything. She bit her lip and tried not to cry. 'I'm sorry I was kind of ignoring you before.'

'Like I said. Daft, not evil.'

Mamie sniffed, which turned unexpectedly into a semi-giggle.

'Sorry.'

'You're forgiven. So. Want to go to Starbucks? Or are you rushing home to chat to a psycho?'

This time her giggle was a little hysterical. Just as well the bubble was still intact. It would break eventually, Mamie supposed, but maybe it wouldn't be so bad. Bearable, if Nicky would stick around. She snuck her arm through Nicky's.

'I want to go to Starbucks, you rude cow. You're buying.'

If you enjoyed reading *No Way!*, look out for other titles in the *On The Wire!* series:

You Can Do it! by Jill Atkins

He's the school's star football player and all round popular guy. Jack's impatient to make the most of his activity week in Snowdonia - but then tragedy strikes. How does he cope when his world is suddenly upended?

No Way! by Sue Vyner

Jessie's life is perfect just as it is: her moody and violent dad has finally left, and now it's just the three of them: her mum, her sister and Jessie. Then Mum brings a new man home. Jessie doesn't want anything to change. But is she making a big mistake?

Seeing Red by Jill Atkins

Vicky this, Vicky that! It's always the same - and Vicky can't stand it for a second longer. So she packs her bags and leaves the nagging behind. But while life on the streets provides welcome relief from her parents, it brings new dangers and hard lessons to be learnt.